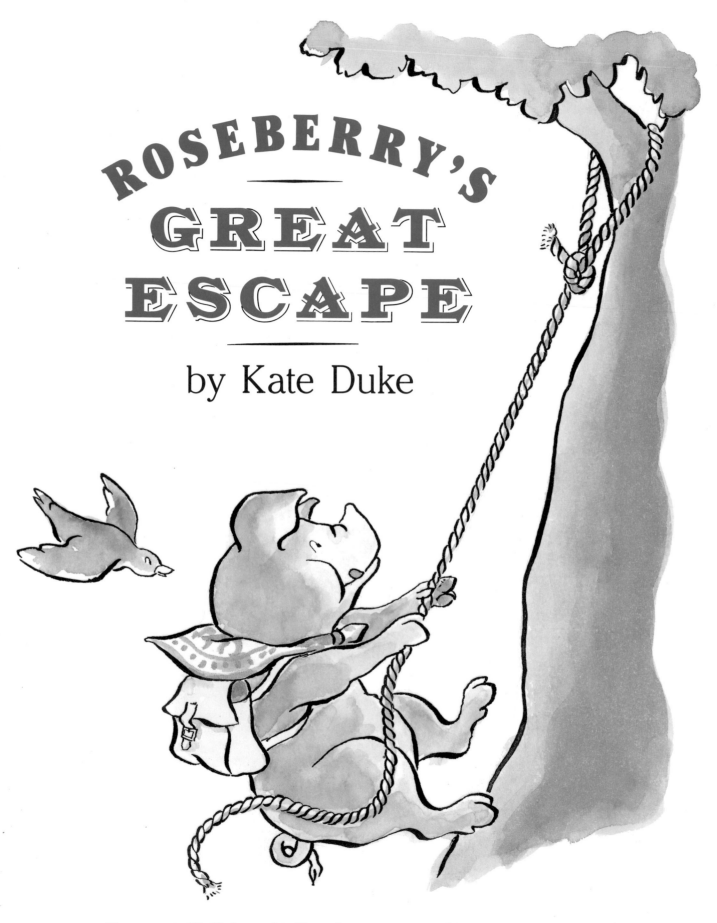

ROSEBERRY'S
GREAT
ESCAPE

by Kate Duke

Dutton Children's Books   New York

With special thanks
to Aesop

Published in the United States by Dutton Children's Books,
a division of Penguin Books USA Inc.

Published simultaneously in Canada by
Fitzhenry & Whiteside Limited, Toronto

Designer: Martha Rago

Printed in Hong Kong by South China Printing Co.
First Edition   10 9 8 7 6 5 4 3 2 1

Library of Congress Cataloging-in-Publication Data

Duke, Kate.
  Roseberry's great escape / by Kate Duke.—1st American ed.
     p.   cm.
  Summary: Tired of traveling from one adventure to the next,
Roseberry the pig finds peace and contentment living with a flock
of sheep until he meets the flock's ham-loving shepherd.
  ISBN 0-525-44597-8
  [1. Pigs—Fiction.   2. Adventure and adventurers—Fiction.]
I. Title.   89-37847
PZ7.D886   Ro 1990   CIP
[E]—dc20   AC

Once upon a time there was a pig named Roseberry. Roseberry liked adventures. With his pack on his back, he roamed the wild places of the countryside, doing things ordinary pigs never dreamed of.

He took flying lessons from the birds,

swam in the water with the fish,

and dug under the ground with the moles and badgers.

Roseberry was always ready to try anything.

And he was such a friendly pig that everyone liked him wherever he went.

Still, there were times when Roseberry had to admit that being out in the world was not much fun. Sometimes he got lost,

sometimes he had to eat things that didn't look very tasty,

and sometimes he got caught in the rain with no
place to stay.

So one especially cold, soggy day, he wondered
if he should give up adventuring. What I need, he
thought, is a nice, comfortable home and a
comfortable, ordinary life.

The next day Roseberry set out to look for a place to make his home. He walked and walked and finally came to a green meadow where some sheep were grazing, watched over by their shepherd.

"Here's a pleasant scene," he said. "Maybe this would be a good place to settle down."

Roseberry decided to find out what life in the meadow was like. How kind the shepherd is! How devoted! he said to himself.

"What fun to be a sheep," Roseberry sighed. He
wished he could join right in.

And the longer he watched, the better he liked
what he saw.

Finally he made a great decision. He would give
up adventures forever and join the shepherd's flock.
"This is the life for me!" he cried. "A peaceful
meadow to live in and a shepherd to look after
my every need! What more could
a pig want?"

With that, he jumped up and introduced himself
to the shepherd. "What's this?" the shepherd cried.
"I'm in luck! There's nothing I like better than a fat
little pig!"

To Roseberry's delight, the shepherd at once
began to treat him like one of his flock.

But alas! Roseberry soon began to fear that something was wrong. "Friends," he said to the sheep, "does it seem to you that events are taking an unusual turn?"

"Don't be silly," said the sheep. "Our shepherd always knows what he's doing. Look how fluffy and white he keeps us."

But Roseberry didn't think the shepherd was planning to make *him* fluffy and white. And sure enough, before he could say another word,

he found himself in a pot of trouble!

"Let me out! Let me out!" he squealed from inside the pot. But the sheep were no help at all.

"Stop making such a racket!" they said. "The shepherd's probably just going to give you a bath. He's always giving *us* baths."

Roseberry didn't believe this for a minute. He
realized he must take matters into his own hooves.
In a flash he was off.

"Stop that pig!" shouted the shepherd.

"Come back, pig!" bleated the sheep.

Roseberry kept running. "Help! Help!" he shouted as he ran.

This time his cries were answered. His old friends were ready to help him escape.

But the shepherd was close behind. There wasn't
a moment to spare. Roseberry thought of a plan.
"Quick!" he cried. "We've got to hurry!"

The shepherd was gaining on him. "I'll get you, pig!" he shouted. Boldly Roseberry made a leap.

He was safe! Roseberry breathed a sigh of relief and, with a grateful heart, he thanked his friends.

Roseberry was glad to be back in the great wide
world. He knew he would never again want to give
up the wandering life. "Meadows and shepherds
may be good for sheep, but they are not necessarily
good for a pig," he said. "A home is where you *feel*
at home, and where you are among friends." And he
thought happily of the adventures that lay ahead.

9